For my parents, who always
encouraged my creativity.
–TK

To John and Eleanor, for always encouraging my
imagination and supporting my love of the arts
–JH

little bee books
an imprint of Bonnier Publishing USA

251 Park Avenue South, New York, NY 10010
Text copyright © 2018 by Tracey Kyle
Illustrations copyright © 2018 by Joshua Heinsz
Manufactured in China   HUH 0418
First Edition 10 9 8 7 6 5 4 3 2 1
ISBN 978-1-4998-0544-4

Library of Congress Cataloging-in-Publication Data
Names: Kyle, Tracey, author. | Heinsz, Joshua, illustrator.
Title: A paintbrush for Paco / by Tracey Kyle; illustrated by Joshua Heinsz.
Description: First edition. | New York, NY: Little Bee Books, [2018]
Summary: Paco cannot seem to concentrate during class, but when his teacher takes him to the art room,
he revels in the colors and the opportunity to paint. Includes author's note and glossary of Spanish words.
Identifiers: LCCN 2017023551 | Subjects: | CYAC: Stories in rhyme. | AttentionFiction. | SchoolsFiction.
| PaintingFiction. | Hispanic AmericansFiction. | Classification: LCC PZ8.3.K984 Pai 2018
| DDC [E]dc23 | LC record available at https://lccn.loc.gov/2017023551

littlebeebooks.com
bonnierpublishingusa.com

A Paintbrush for Paco

WRITTEN BY
TRACEY KYLE

ILLUSTRATED BY
JOSHUA HEINSZ

WITHDRAWN

little bee books

Paco gazed out at the late-morning sun.

He wondered why recess had not yet begun.

He wanted to go to **el campo** and play,

and act like a matador shouting **"¡olé!"**

He thought about **fútbol**, and scoring a **"¡Gol!"**

He wanted to run in the sun. . . .

"¡Hace sol!"

He longed for his lunch

with **manzanas** and cheese.

He yearned for a nap underneath the big trees.

"Paco?" he heard. It was **el profesor**.

"Let's follow the lesson," he said, **"por favor."**

Paco blushed, turning a light shade of red.

He sank in his chair and he lowered his head.

But one hour later, he could not sit still.

He daydreamed and looked

out the window until . . .

he lifted his **lápiz** and started to draw

the life in his **pueblo**, the world that he saw.

He colored **montañas** that stretched to the sky,

with **pájaros** swooping down low, flying high.

He doodled his picture and made a **retrato**,

with Mami and Papi and Pancho, his **gato**.

"¡Paco! **¡Caramba!**" Profesor cried.

He leaned on the desk, and his eyes opened wide.

"Paco," he whispered,

"you must come with me.

There's a **salón de clase**

I need you to see."

Later, they walked down the hall to a room
with easels and brushes and colors in bloom.

Pink, **rosado**. Purple, **morado**.

A fiery orange, **anaranjado**.

verde, the green in a vine of ripe grapes.

Rojo, the red in the matadors' capes.

Azul, the blue in a beautiful sky.

Blanco, the white in the clouds floating by.

Amarillo, the rays of the sun shining bright.

Negro, the black of el campo at night.

Next, Paco picked out a brush, **un pincel**.

He chose a few paints and he mixed them up well.

He painted and painted
and when he was through,
his heart burst in green,
yellow, orange, and blue.

Profesor clapped and said, "**¡Qué talentoso!**

Your artwork is brilliant and **maravilloso!**"

Paco was grateful and felt so **contento**.

He knew this was such an important **momento**.

Paco looked up at his proud profesor, who said,

"You're a painter! **¡Tú eres pintor!**"

Later that night, Paco crawled into bed,

a palette of colors swirling in his head.

**Negro y blanco,
azul y rosado.
Rojo y verde
y anaranjado.**

He fell asleep holding the brush to his heart,

and dreamed of the new world he'd found full of art.

Author's Note

The idea for *A Paintbrush for Paco* grew out of my many years as a middle- and high-school language teacher. In every class, I taught a student like Paco, the well-meaning but restless daydreamer who can't wait to get out and about. Middle-school students, in particular, are a jittery bunch, and I soon found myself in a room full of not one, but six or seven kids like Paco! As a strategy to engage my students and channel their energy, I bought a set of mini white boards. They loved using them to interact with the lessons and it helped them focus better. I began to design more creative projects to assess them, and discovered that after hours of electronic devices, they relished the chance to express themselves with crayons and markers. The students were engaged and learning.

Paco's Latino culture fuels his creativity. The bullfights, nature, food, family, and, of course, soccer are the inspirations for his paintings. Many a parent or teacher has a child like Paco in his or her world, and it's up to us to foster that growing talent and allow them space to be inspired.

GLOSSARY

Spanish Word	English Word	Pronunciation
amarillo	yellow	ah-mah-REE-oh
anaranjado	orange	ah-nah-rahn-HA-doh
azul	blue	ah-SOOL
blanco	white	BLAHN-koh
campo	countryside	KAM-poh
caramba	(expression of surprise)	cah-RAHM-ba
contento	happy	kohn-TEHN-toh
fútbol	soccer	FOOT-bohl
gato	cat	GAH-toh
gol	goal	GOHL
hace sol	it's sunny out	AH-say SOHL
lápiz	pencil	lah-PEES
manzanas	apples	mahn-SAHN-ahs
maravilloso	marvelous	mah-rah-bee-YOH-soh
momento	moment	moh-MEHN-toh
montañas	mountains	mohn-TAHN-yahs
morado	purple	moh-RAH-doh
negro	black	NEH-groh
olé	hooray	oh-LEH
pájaros	birds	PAH-ha-rohs
pincel	paintbrush	peen-SELL
por favor	please	poor fah-BOHR
profesor	teacher	proh-feh-SOHR
pueblo	town	PWEH-bloh
qué talentoso	how talented	kay tah-len-TOH-soh
retrato	portrait	reh-TRAH-toh
rojo	red	RROH-hoh
rosado	pink	roh-SAH-doh
salón de clase	classroom	sah-LOHN day CLAH-say
tú eres pintor	you're a painter	too eh-rehs peen-TOHR
verde	green	BEHR-day

31901063290748